Summertime

FROM
Porgy and Bess

by GEORGE GERSHWIN,
DuBOSE *and* DOROTHY HEYWARD,
and IRA GERSHWIN

paintings by MIKE WIMMER

SIMON & SCHUSTER BOOKS FOR YOUNG READERS

Special thanks and gratitude to
Gloria and Jerry Pinkney,
who through their work in children's literature
and their examples as parents and teachers
have given us so much.

— M.W.

SIMON & SCHUSTER
BOOKS FOR YOUNG READERS

An imprint of Simon & Schuster Children's Publishing Division

1230 Avenue of the Americas

New York, New York 10020

Summertime © 1999 based on the Composition "Summertime"

from the folk opera entitled *Porgy and Bess* by George Gershwin,

DuBose and Dorothy Heyward and Ira Gershwin

© 1935 (renewed 1962) George Gershwin Music,

Ira Gershwin Music and The DuBose and Dorothy Heyward Memorial Fund

Used by permission.

Illustrations copyright © 1999 by Mike Wimmer

Book design by Heather Wood

The text for this book is set in Horley Old Style Semi-Bold Italic.

The paintings were rendered in oil paint on linen canvas;

they were inspired by the work of Winslow Homer.

Printed and bound in the United States of America

1 3 5 7 9 10 8 6 4 2

ISBN 0-689-80719-8

Library of Congress Catalog Card Number: 98-88194

Elijah and Lauren,
I sang this song to you every night;
now I give it to you forever.

— M. W.

Summertime

and the livin' is easy,

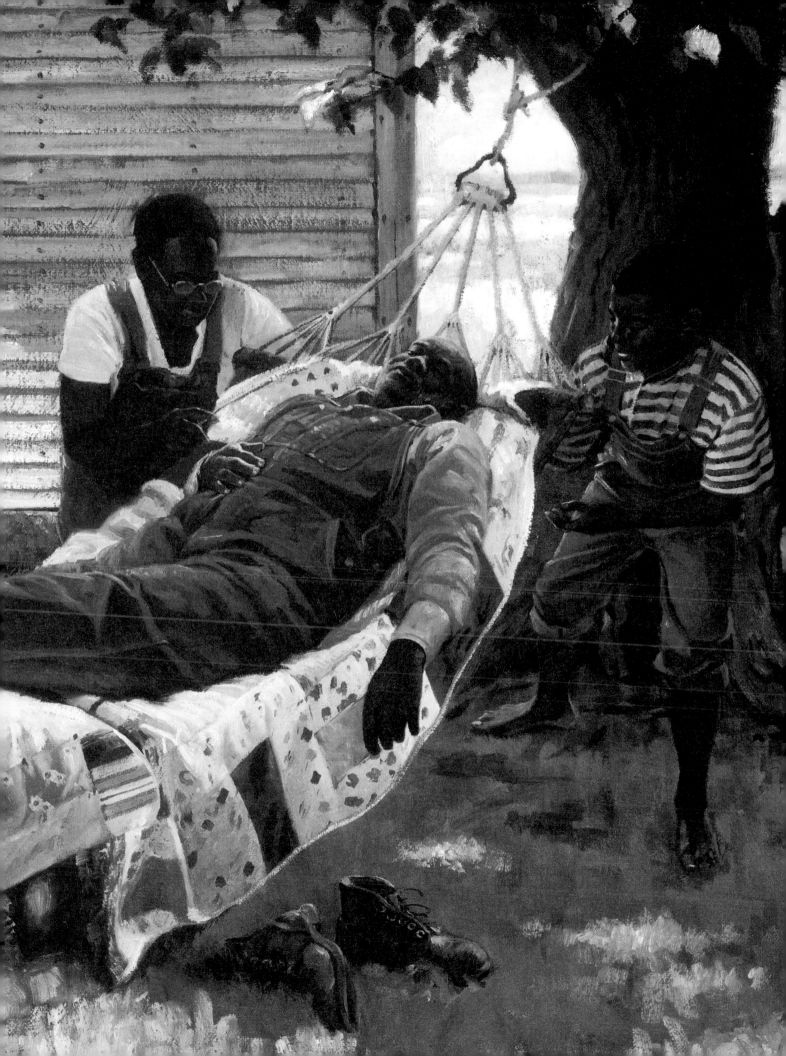

Fish are jumpin',

and the cotton is high.

Oh your daddy's rich,

*and your ma
is good lookin',*

*So hush,
little baby,
don't you cry.*

One of these mornin's

you're goin' to
rise up singin',

Then you'll spread your wings

*and you'll take
to the sky.*

But till that mornin'

there's a nothin' can harm you

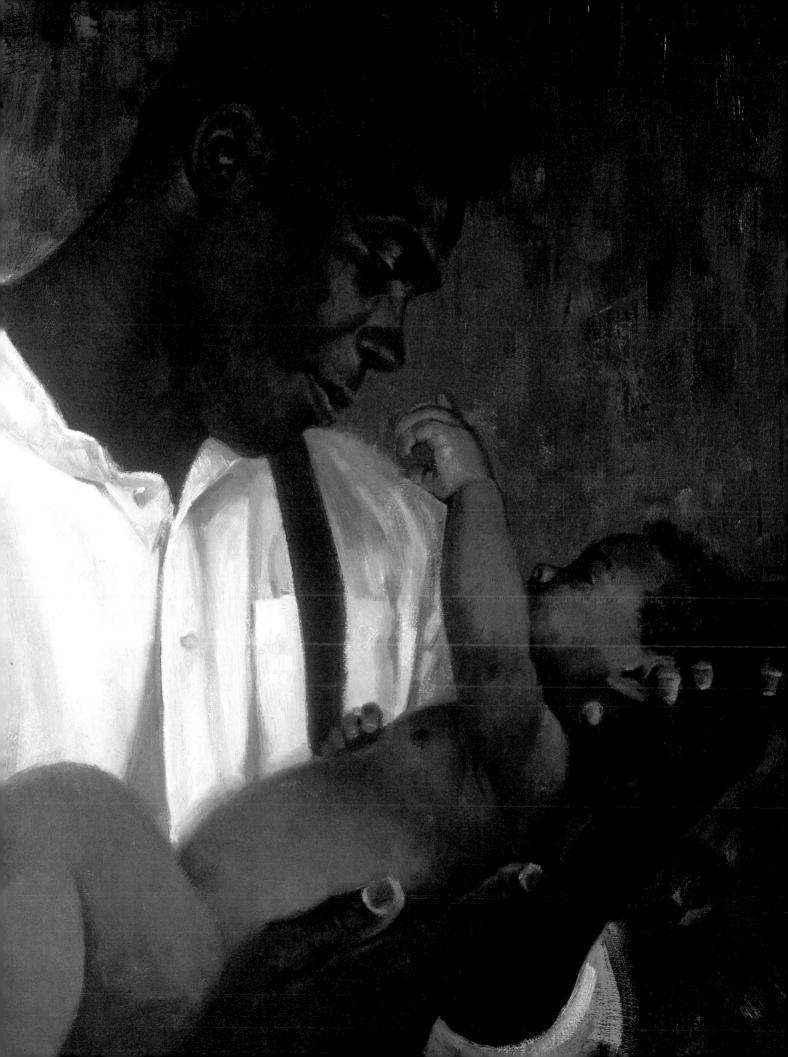

with Daddy and Mama standin' by.

Summertime

FROM *Porgy and Bess*

by GEORGE GERSHWIN, DuBOSE *and* DOROTHY HEYWARD, *and* IRA GERSHWIN

Moderato

Bm6

Sum-mer time _____ and the liv-in' is eas - y, _____ Fish are

Em7   F#   C#7   F#   F#7

jump-in', _____ and the cot - ton is high. _____ Oh your

Bm6

dad-dy's rich, _ and your ma is good look - in', _____ So

D   Bm   E   A9sus   Bm

hush, lit-tle ba-by, don't you cry. _____ One of these

Bm6

morn-in's you're goin' to rise _ up sing - in', _____ Then you'll

Em7   F#   C#7   F#   F#7

spread your wings _ and you'll take to the sky. _____ But till that

Bm6

morn-in' _____ there's a noth-in' can harm you _____ with

D   Bm   E   A9sus   Bm

Dad - dy and Ma - ma stand - in' by. _____